THE LITTLE MERMAID

Story written by Neil Morris
**Based upon The Walt Disney Company's
film of the same name**

**Hippo Books
Scholastic Children's Books
London**

Scholastic Children's Books
Scholastic Publications Ltd,
7-9 Pratt Street, London NW1 0AE, UK

Scholastic Inc.,
730 Broadway, New York, NY 10003, USA

Scholastic Canada Ltd,
123 Newkirk Road, Richmond Hill,
Ontario, Canada L4C 3G5

Ashton Scholastic Pty Ltd,
P O Box 579, Gosford, New South Wales,
Australia

Ashton Scholastic Ltd,
Private Bag 1, Penrose, Auckland,
New Zealand

Published by Scholastic Publications Ltd, 1990
by arrangement with the Walt Disney Company

ISBN 0 590 76360 1

Made and Printed in Spain by Mateu Cromo,
Madrid

10 9 8 7 6 5

It was a blustery day, and the sea was choppy. Young Prince Eric was enjoying his voyage on the big sailing ship. "Isn't this great?" he said happily. "The salty sea air, the wind in your face – the perfect day to be at sea!"

Eric's big woolly sheepdog barked in agreement. But the prince's guardian, Sir Grimsby, was not so happy. Perhaps this was because he was feeling seasick!

The sailors were certainly enjoying themselves. "A fine strong wind and a following sea," yelled one. "King Triton must be in a friendly mood today."

"King Triton? Who's that?" asked Eric.

"Why, ruler of the merpeople, lad," an old sea dog replied, taking fish from his bulging nets.

"Nautical nonsense!" Grimsby sneered queasily.

The old sea dog held up one of his fish. "But it ain't nonsense," he said. "Down in the depths of the ocean they live, in mysterious fathoms below!" And as he spoke, the fish wriggled out of his hands and dived over the side of the ship.

Down and down the fish swam, till at last it reached the very bottom of the ocean. Here was the merpeople's glittering palace, and they were gathering today for a special event. It was the day of the mermaids' grand concert.

With a blare of royal trumpets, King Triton himself entered on a chariot drawn by dolphins. He was followed by a small crab, the concert conductor. "I'm really looking forward to this, Sebastian," Triton told the crab.

"It will be the finest concert I have ever conducted, Your Majesty," Sebastian said confidently. "Your daughters will be spectacular."

"Especially my little Ariel," smiled the king, "in her very first performance."

As music filled the ocean, three large shells opened, each one carrying two of Triton's beautiful daughters. The six mermaids introduced themselves one by one to the audience. "Aquata," one sang, "Andrina," sang another, "Arista," "Attina," "Adella," "Alana," until at last they came to the seventh sister. The mermaids held out their hands to a fourth, beautiful shell. "In her musical debut," they sang, "our little sister, Ariel!"

The shell slowly opened, to reveal . . . nothing! The shell was empty! The audience gasped, Sebastian looked shocked, and King Triton's face grew red with anger. Then he roared, "ARIEL!"

The king's voice echoed through the ocean depths. But
Ariel did not hear the call. She was far away, playing with
her friend, a plump fish called Flounder. She had found a
sunken ship on the seabed, and was busy exploring.

Swimming into one of the ship's cabins, Ariel picked up a
fork. "Oh my gosh," said the pretty little mermaid. "Have
you ever seen anything so wonderful?" Ariel was fascinated
by everyday things from the human world, and she was
collecting them in her bag.

But before Flounder could answer, a dark shadow fell across the cabin. "A sh . . . shark!" he stammered, swimming into Ariel's arms.

Suddenly, the ship began to shake, and the shark burst through the side! Ariel grabbed her bag and began swimming as fast as her tail could push her. Flounder followed, and there was a frantic chase up and down the ship. The shark snapped at Flounder, its jaws barely missing the little fish.

At last, the two friends escaped from the ship, as the shark got caught up in the anchor. Ariel and Flounder swam swiftly to the surface of the sea.

There, perched on a rock, was a rather rumpled-looking seagull. "Hey, Scuttle," Ariel called. "Look what we found!" She opened her bag.

"Human stuff, huh?" said the seagull, peering curiously into the bag. "Now, let me see," he pulled out the fork. "Ah," said Scuttle, "a dinglehopper!" He showed Ariel how a fork was used by humans to comb their hair! Next he brought a pipe out of the bag. "Now, I haven't seen one of these for years," the seagull said. "This is a snarfblatt, invented by humans to make fine music."

Ariel looked startled. "Music!" she cried. "Oh my gosh, the concert! I forgot all about it. Father will kill me!" She dived underwater and headed as fast as she could for the merkingdom.

As Ariel and Flounder hurried home, they had no idea they were being watched. Ursula, the fat sea witch with a blubbery, octopus body, was following their every move in her magic pool of light. She had once lived with the merpeople, but had been banished long ago. "Yes, hurry home, princess," the witch sneered. "You are the key to Triton's undoing!"

When Ariel arrived at her father's palace, she did her best to apologize. Flounder tried to help. "It wasn't her fault," he explained. "First this shark chased us . . . and we tried to . . . but we couldn't . . . and he . . . and I knew we were safe . . . then this seagull came. . ."

"Seagull?" roared Triton. "That means you went up to the surface again. You might have been caught by one of those fish-eating barbarians!"

"Daddy, they're not barbarians!" said Ariel. "And besides, I'm sixteen years old. I'm not a child any more."

"Not another word," said Triton firmly. "As long as you live under my ocean, you'll obey my rules!" The king knew he had to take action. He sent his daughter away, and told an unhappy Sebastian to keep a watchful eye on her.

The crab scuttled along, hurrying to catch up with Ariel. He found her in a shell-encrusted grotto, where she was showing Flounder her collection of human objects. Sebastian knew that Ariel would be in a lot of trouble if her father ever knew of this collection, and he begged her to come home with him. But as he spoke, a huge shadow passed slowly over the grotto. Ariel swam straight up to the surface.

There, the mermaid was enchanted to see Prince Eric's ship. The sailors were singing, dancing and letting off fireworks. It was the prince's birthday. Sebastian and Flounder followed, as Ariel went right up to the ship to get a better look. Even Scuttle flew over to watch the party. Ariel couldn't take her eyes off Eric. "I've never seen a human this close before," she whispered to the seagull. "He's so handsome!"

As she spoke, lightning flashed through the sky. A storm blew up quickly, and soon the ship was tossing and heaving. Ariel could only watch helplessly as lightning struck the ship's mast, setting it alight. The fire quickly spread towards a powder keg, and suddenly there was a huge explosion. Eric was flung into the churning sea. Quick as a flash, Ariel darted down to save him as he sank. She pulled him to the surface, and swam with him to shore.

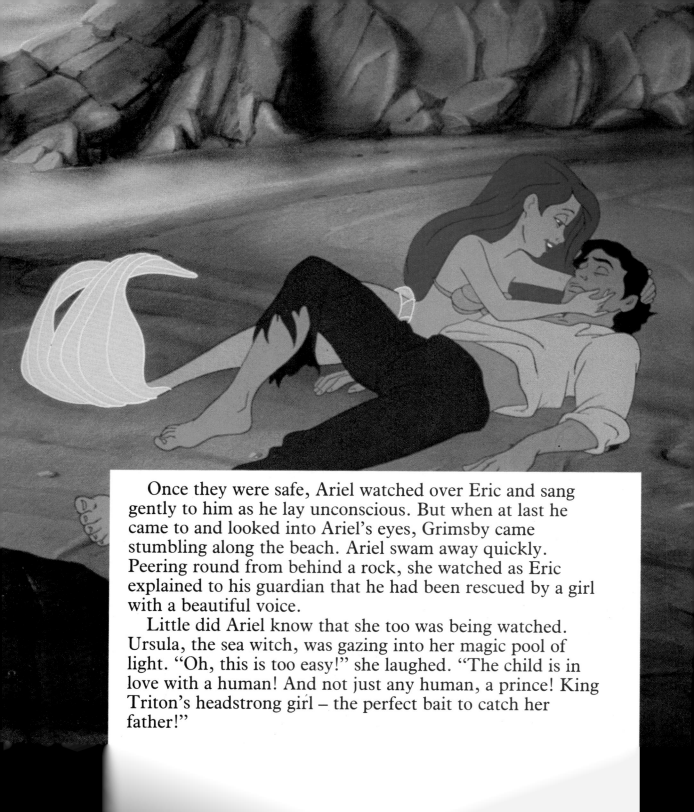

Once they were safe, Ariel watched over Eric and sang gently to him as he lay unconscious. But when at last he came to and looked into Ariel's eyes, Grimsby came stumbling along the beach. Ariel swam away quickly. Peering round from behind a rock, she watched as Eric explained to his guardian that he had been rescued by a girl with a beautiful voice.

Little did Ariel know that she too was being watched. Ursula, the sea witch, was gazing into her magic pool of light. "Oh, this is too easy!" she laughed. "The child is in love with a human! And not just any human, a prince! King Triton's headstrong girl – the perfect bait to catch her father!"

King Triton knew nothing of Ursula's evil plans. But he was very worried. There was a rumour in the palace that Ariel was in love . . . and that she had made contact with the human world. The king looked everywhere for Ariel, and found her at last in her secret grotto.

Ariel saw that her father was angry and tried to hide behind a huge statue.

"Is it true you rescued a human from drowning?" the king boomed.

"Daddy, I had to," Ariel replied.

"Contact between the human world and the merworld is strictly forbidden," the king said sternly.

"But you don't even know him," Ariel protested.

"I don't have to know him," the king bellowed. "Humans are all the same – spineless, savage, harpooning fisheaters!"

"But Daddy, I love him," Ariel said quietly.

"No!" roared her father, raising his trident and aiming it at her collection of treasures. Sparks shot through the grotto, and the human objects were shattered. King Triton swam off in a rage, leaving Ariel sobbing alone.

But she was not alone for long. The sea witch's evil eels, Flotsam and Jetsam, came slithering along. "Don't be scared," they hissed. "We know someone who can make all your dreams come true. Just imagine, you and your prince, together forever."

Ariel didn't trust these slimy eels, and yet she found herself following them. She would do anything to be with Prince Eric.

The witch was delighted to see her. "Come in, my child," she said. "You're here because you have a thing for this prince fellow. Well, there's only one way to get what you want – become human yourself!"

"Can you do that?" Ariel gasped.

"My dear, I live to help poor merfolk like you," the witch cackled. "Here's the deal. I will turn you into a human for three days. But before the sun sets on the third day, your prince must give you a kiss of true love. If that happens, you'll stay human forever. But if it doesn't, you'll turn back into a mermaid and belong to me!" Ursula smiled an evil smile. "Oh, and one more thing – the question of payment. I'm not asking much, just a token really. What I want from you, my dear, is . . . your voice!"

Ariel was horrified, as Ursula magically produced a contract for her to sign. But she wanted to be with Eric so much, that she signed straight away. Ursula spoke some magic words over her witch's cauldron. A potion bubbled and steamed. "Now sing!" she commanded.

As Ariel began to sing, ghostly hands rose from the cauldron and drifted towards her. They took a glowing sphere from her throat and gave it to the witch. It was her voice!

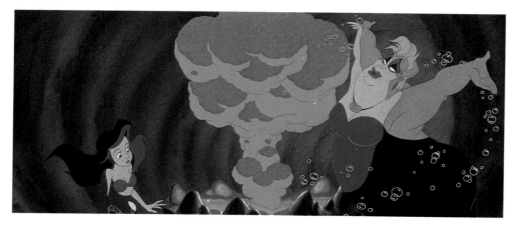

Ariel watched in amazement as her tail started to turn into legs. But when the change was complete, she began to panic. Now that she was human, she could drown! She struggled towards the surface.

Sebastian and Flounder had been watching the whole episode with the sea witch in terror. Now they rushed to Ariel's rescue and helped her to reach the seashore. There she quickly recovered and started kicking her new legs and wiggling her new toes. Scuttle flew over, grabbed a torn piece of sail that had washed up on the beach, and wrapped it round Ariel.

As they admired Ariel's new dress, a dog came bounding along the beach. It was Prince Eric's big sheepdog, and he barked and barked when he saw Ariel. Eric soon came to see what all the fuss was about. He had been thinking about the girl with the beautiful voice who saved him from the sea, and at first he thought he recognized her. "You're the one I've been looking for," he said. "What's your name?"

Ariel opened her mouth to reply, but nothing happened – she had no voice! After a while Eric understood. "You can't speak?" he said. "Then you can't be who I thought you were."

Ariel frantically pointed out to sea, trying to make him understand who she was. But she was not yet used to her new legs, and they wobbled beneath her. Eric rushed to help. "Come on," he said kindly, "I'll take you to the castle. You'll be okay." Sebastian quickly jumped up and hid in Ariel's pocket.

At the castle, Ariel was given beautiful new clothes. When she came in to dinner that evening, she looked wonderful. But still the prince didn't realize that she was the one who had saved him. Grimsby, Eric's guardian, was very surprised when Ariel picked a fork up from the table and combed her hair with it. And he was not amused when she blew into his pipe and covered him with soot!

Next morning, Eric took Ariel out in the royal carriage. Sebastian hid in Ariel's pocket again, and watched eagerly, hoping that Eric would kiss her.

From then on, the two young people spent every moment they could together. But the three days granted by the evil sea witch were passing quickly, and still Eric had not kissed Ariel. Now there was only one day left! Sebastian decided he had to do something . . .

When the prince took Ariel on a boat trip across a beautiful blue lagoon, Sebastian had an idea. He called together a group of colourful fish and sea creatures who swam around the boat and sang softly to Eric. "Go on, kiss the girl," they sang, "kiss the girl!"

Eric leaned towards Ariel and gazed into her eyes. She smiled at him, and they were just about to kiss, when the boat suddenly rocked and they fell into the water.

In her lair, the sea witch was watching events through her pool of light. "That was a close one," she laughed. Now she was getting quite worried. She would do everything she could to keep Eric and Ariel apart. "It's time Ursula took matters into her own tentacles," she snarled and sat down in front of her mirror. Grabbing the shell that held Ariel's voice, she drank a potion from her steamy cauldron. She began to twitch and writhe. Her octopus body was changing. Ursula turned into a beautiful young woman!

That night, Prince Eric heard someone singing in the sea mist. He knew he had heard that voice before. It had to be the girl who had saved him from the shipwreck. He ran quickly to the beach, and there, walking towards him through the mist, was a beautiful young woman.

Next morning, Ariel was woken by loud seagull cries. Scuttle was at her window. "Congratulations!" the seagull squawked. "The whole town's buzzing with the news. The prince is getting married this afternoon!"

Ariel couldn't believe her ears. She had never felt so happy in her life, and she ran out of the room to find the prince. But then her world fell apart. She saw Prince Eric in the hall with another young woman. He was making arrangements with Grimsby. "Vanessa and I wish to be married as soon as possible," Eric said, smiling at his bride-to-be. "The wedding ship will leave at sunset."

Preparations were made at once. The wedding ship was decorated with banners and, as it left the pier, all Ariel could do was sit and cry. The ship made its way out to sea, followed by a single seagull. It was Scuttle, who had come to wish Ariel luck. But when he looked into the princess's cabin, he saw that the new princess was not to be Ariel. And when the young woman looked into her mirror, Scuttle saw, with horror, that a different face smiled back at her. It was the face of Ursula, the sea witch!

Scuttle flew to the pier and told Ariel what he had seen. Sebastian knew at once what to do. "Flounder," he ordered, "get Ariel to that boat as fast as your fins will carry you. I must tell King Triton. Scuttle, you find a way to stall the wedding."

Scuttle squawked the alarm. He was quickly surrounded by birds, seals and other creatures, all ready to help. When they arrived at the ship, the wedding ceremony was underway. The birds quickly flew at Vanessa. "Get away from me," she screeched, "you slimy little. . . ." A seal tossed her high in the air. Prince Eric was shocked at Vanessa's nasty voice, and just then he saw Ariel climbing onto the ship.

Scuttle tried to tear Vanessa's necklace from her, and at last the chain broke and the seashell fell to the deck and shattered. The glowing sphere that held Ariel's voice floated back towards her throat. "Eric," Ariel said weakly.

The prince was startled. "You can talk," he said to Ariel. "You're the one. It was you all the time!"

"Get away from her!" Vanessa snapped. Ariel's legs were slowly changing into a tail! As the others watched in horror, Vanessa laughed and turned back into the octopus shape of Ursula, the sea witch. "You're too late!" she screeched, grabbing Ariel and diving overboard.

They plunged underwater. But suddenly Ursula came face to face with King Triton, who had been warned by Sebastian. "Let her go!" Triton boomed.

"Not a chance," laughed the witch. "She's mine now! But of course I might be willing to exchange her for someone even better." As she spoke, the contract that Ariel had signed floated down before Triton. "Do we have a deal?" asked the witch.

Triton didn't hesitate. But as soon as he signed, he shrivelled into a captive sea plant. Ursula picked up his crown, and laughed victoriously. But as she did so, a harpoon shot through the water and struck her on the arm. Ursula looked round in horror. It was Eric!

Eric rushed to the surface for air, and Ariel streaked after him. There they embraced, but they were not safe yet. Eight huge tentacles rose out of the water. "You pitiful fools," screamed the witch. "You can't escape me now. I am ruler of all oceans!"

To show her power, Ursula waved the trident to make a whirlpool. It was so strong that it even stirred up wrecked ships at the bottom of the ocean. As his old ship rose to the surface, Eric clambered aboard. He stood at the helm and aimed the ship straight at Ursula. The witch saw the ship too late, as it ploughed through the waves and crashed right into her. She writhed and squirmed, and soon nothing was left of her but a mass of black ooze.

The royal trident sank to the seabed, and magically turned the captive sea plant back into Triton, king of the merpeople. As the seas calmed, King Triton saw Ariel and Eric together in the distance. He realized how much they loved each other. "I suppose there's just one problem left," he said to Sebastian, "and that's how much I'm going to miss her."

Without another word he pointed the trident at his daughter. A magic light shot through the water to the rock where she was sitting. When it reached her, her mermaid's tail turned into legs.

Ariel and Prince Eric were married that very day. All the merpeople gathered to wish the new princess well.

King Triton swam towards the ship and rose out of the water to give his daughter a farewell embrace.

    As the ship sailed towards the horizon, Ariel blew her father a kiss and waved happily to her sisters and all her friends. Her dreams had all come true. She had found her prince, and the little mermaid was human at last.